FREDERICK WARNE
Penguin Young Readers Group
An Imprint of Penguin Random House LLC

Penguin supports copyright. Copyright fuels creativity, encourages diverse voices, promotes free speech, and creates a vibrant culture. Thank you for buying an authorized edition of this book and for complying with copyright laws by not reproducing, scanning, or distributing any part of it in any form without permission. You are supporting writers and allowing Penguin to continue to publish books for every reader.

First published in the United States of America in 2017 by Frederick Warne, an imprint of Penguin Random House LLC, 345 Hudson Street, New York, New York 10014.

Manufactured in China

ISBN 9780241301340

10 9 8 7 6 5 4 3 2 1

LOVE

from PETER RABBIT

in the
WORLD so
BIG
and
WIDE,

WHEN THE
SUN
begins
to hide.

LOVE
IS HOW YOU
make
me
laugh

WHENEVER
times get
tough,

IT'S ALL
the smiles
YOU GIVE ME,

I WILL *never have* ENOUGH.

LOVE
IS HOW
you hold
my hand

WHEN
I FEEL
*a little
lost,*

IT'S A *warm and cozy* FEELING

WHEN OUTSIDE
THERE'S
SNOW
and
FROST.

LOVE
will

WHEN WE ARE together,

EVERYTHING *just feels* RIGHT.

SO *finally,*
THERE IS
ONE *thing*

THAT I WOULD *like to do...*

IT'S TO
GIVE MY
hugs and
kisses

and to
SAY THAT...